MW00966180

The adventures of otto

Look Out!
A Storm!

David Milgrim

Ready-to-Read

Simon Spotlight

New York   London   Toronto   Sydney   New Delhi

For Chris and Simone

And for everyone
who has ever been in a bad mood

SIMON SPOTLIGHT
An imprint of Simon & Schuster Children's Publishing Division
1230 Avenue of the Americas, New York, New York 10020
This Simon Spotlight edition July 2019
Copyright © 2019 by David Milgrim
All rights reserved, including the right of reproduction in whole or in part in any form.
SIMON SPOTLIGHT, READY-TO-READ, and colophon are registered trademarks
of Simon & Schuster, Inc.
For information about special discounts for bulk purchases, please contact
Simon & Schuster Special Sales at 1-866-506-1949
or business@simonandschuster.com.
Manufactured in the United States of America 0519 LAK
2 4 6 8 10 9 7 5 3 1
Library of Congress Cataloging-in-Publication Data
Names: Milgrim, David, author, illustrator.
Title: Look out! a storm! / David Milgrim.
Description: New York : Simon Spotlight, 2019. | Series: The adventures of Otto | Series:
Ready-to-read. Pre-level 1 | Summary: "Otto the robot and his friends contend with a storm"—
Provided by publisher. | Description based on print version record and CIP data provided by
publisher; resource not viewed.|Identifiers: LCCN 2018043057 (print) |
LCCN 2018049074 (eBook) | ISBN 9781534441972 (hardback) | ISBN 9781534441965 (pbk) |
ISBN 9781534441989 (eBook) | Subjects: | CYAC: Robots—Fiction. | Monkeys—Fiction. |
Storms—Fiction. | BISAC: JUVENILE FICTION / Readers / Beginner. | JUVENILE FICTION /
Humorous Stories. | JUVENILE FICTION / Robots. Classification: LCC PZ7.M5955 (eBook) |
LCC PZ7.M5955 Loo 2019 (print) | DDC [E]—dc23
LC record available at https://lccn.loc.gov/2018043057

Look, Olly is in
a bad mood.

Otto does not know.

See Otto
give Olly a
big hello.

Now Otto knows.

See Olly go.

See Otto go.

Oh no!

Look out, Flip and Flop!

Oops!

Look!

Now Flip and
Flop are in a
bad mood too.

See Flip and
Flop go.

See Olly go.

See Otto go!

Go, go, go!

Go, Olly, go!

See the storm go.

Look! Olly is in
a good mood!